The Dolphin Rescue

A Miniworld Adventure

The Dolphin Rescue
A Miniworld Adventure

Story by
Emily Adams, Lindsey Boynton,
Sophie Boynton, Taylor Vahey
With Jan Hall

Illustrated by Bobbi LeBonte

Spartacus Media Enterprises™
Metro Boston, Massachusetts

The Dolphin Rescue, A Miniworld Adventure
Story by Emily Adams, Lindsey Boynton, Sophie Boynton, and Taylor Vahey; with Jan Hall;
illustrated by Bobbi LeBonte; cabin art by Morgan Potter. Miniworld is a creation of the publisher, Spartacus
Media Enterprises™.

Send all inquiries to: Spartacus Media Enterprises, P. O. Box 81315, Wellesley Hills, MA 02481
info@spartacusmedia.com (email correspondence preferred)

For paperback or e-book ordering information, please visit www.miniworld.net

ISBN of printed book, 978-1-7323408-0-0
Kindle e-book ISBN 978-1-7323408-2-4

Publisher's Cataloging-In-Publication Data
(Prepared by The Donohue Group, Inc.)

Names: Adams, Emily, 2001- | LeBonte, Bobbi, illustrator.
Title: The dolphin rescue : a Miniworld adventure / story by Emily Adams
    [and 4 others] ; illustrated by Bobbi LeBonte.
Description: Metro Boston, Massachusetts : Spartacus Media Enterprises,
    [2018] | Interest age level: 011-014. | Summary: " … a lively
    adventure in which four teen girls with special powers attempt to help
    change a dolphin fishing drive in Japan. Through their efforts, they
    hope to allow residents to see that dolphins are too smart to be
    harvested by people as food."-- Provided by publisher.
Identifiers: ISBN 9781732340800 (print) |
    ISBN 9781732340824 (Kindle)
Subjects: LCSH: Dolphins--Conservation--Japan--Juvenile fiction. |
    Dolphins--Effect of hunting on--Japan--Juvenile fiction. | Dolphins--
    Psychology--Juvenile fiction. | Teenage girls--Japan--Juvenile fiction.
    | CYAC: Dolphins--Conservation--Japan--Fiction. | Fishing--Japan--
    Fiction. | Dolphins--Psychology--Fiction. | Teenage girls--Japan--
    Fiction. | LCGFT: Action and adventure fiction.
Classification: LCC PZ7.1.A17 Do 2018 (print) | LCC PZ7.1.A17 (ebook) |
    DDC [Fic]--dc23

Printed in the United States of America
1 2 3 4 5 6 7 8 9 22 21 20 19 18

Unless someone like you
cares a whole awful lot,
nothing is going to get better,
it's not.

Dr. Seuss, *The Lorax*

Acknowledgments

We first want to share our deep appreciation to Jan Hall, Bobbi LeBonte, Aunt Carol, Farrah Sing-Peters, and Victoria Kichuk for their loyal commitment to this book.

We also want to thank our parents for their love and support during the process of creating this book.

Dedication

We dedicate this book to all the dolphins who have lost their lives in the dolphin slaughter.

The Girls Behind the Story

(left to right)

Emily Adams

Emily Adams is a junior in high school. She is interested in all art forms and is currently involved in ceramics, studio art, and photography. She loves working with younger kids through work as a swim instructor and tutor.

Lindsey Boynton

Lindsey is a high school junior who has a passion for animal welfare. Lindsey has been a vegan and animal activist for three years. She wants to pursue data science in college. Her favorite activities are taking care of animals, watching her favorite TV shows, and hanging with her best friends.

Taylor Vahey

Taylor is a junior at Bourne High School. She is eager to go off to college soon and study business. In her free time she likes to go out to eat, hang out with her amazing, supportive friends and family, and travel. She is so excited to share her book with you!

Sophie Boynton

Sophie Boynton enjoys studying the sciences and literature. She might become a researcher of chemistry or of outer space. Her favorite activities are gardening, reading, playing the steel pans, and woodland walks.

Foreword

Reading this delight-filled book can help anyone, young or old, recognize how important it is for authors of all ages to imagine a world in which many different living beings can thrive.

Yet Emily, Lindsey, Sophie, and Taylor do even more, bestowing upon each reader the gift of a hopeful future and modeling for today's world that every choice we make can, as Frances Moore Lappe has suggested, "be a celebration of the world we want."

Dr. Paul Waldau

Anthrozoology graduate program, Professor and Director, at Canisius College.

Harvard Law School, Barker Visiting Professor of Animal Law.

Yale, Interdisciplinary Center for Bioethics.

Tufts University School of Veterinary Medicine, former director
of the Center for Animals and Public Policy.

Author of *Animal Studies: An Introduction* (Oxford University Press)

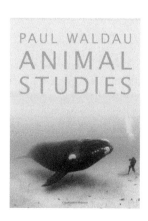

Contents

CHAPTER NINE
What the Hunters Snared

CHAPTER TEN
A Race Against Time

CHAPTER ELEVEN
Town on a Tightrope

CHAPTER TWELVE
Penguin in Peril

EPILOGUE
An Urgent Email from Taro

Prologue

"Special delivery!" a strange man said at Aunt Carol's door, almost too cheerfully. Aunt Carol cautiously peered through the window at the mystery visitor.

I wasn't expecting a package so late on a Sunday evening, Aunt Carol thought with suspicion. Not only was this hour an unusual time for a delivery, but his dark clothing, unsettling grin, and slouched shoulders sent a chill up her spine. She quickly noticed similar men surrounding the yard and shot Taylor a worried glance. Taylor gathered the other three girls and whispered, "It must be a surprise for us. Follow me up to the attic, stay quiet, and stick close together." Thinking ahead, Taylor quickly grabbed their winter coats, and the children rushed up the steep, narrow stairs and climbed into the cold, musty attic. They zipped up their winter coats, excited, hoping that they could still go out and build snowmen after they opened their special delivery package. It was a tradition the six year olds looked forward to all year. Taylor was immediately distracted by an old foggy mirror and began to fix her hair.

Lindsey whined, "Ewww, there's something burning!"

Taylor responded, "That's probably just the cookies."

"Just the cookies!" wailed Sophie. "I hope this package is worth it!"

"I think the delivery is a bunny." Emily guessed.

"I thinks it's a kitty!" Sophie exclaimed.

Taylor was quick to correct her. "The word is think, not thinks, Sophie."

"Same differerence, Taylor!" Sophie responded.

Lindsey, who had been staring out the attic window, piped up, asking, "Why is Aunt Carol down there beating up the delivery guy? That's not very kind. I want my package," she whined.

Taylor and Sophie ignored Lindsey and discussed possibilities about the mystery package.

"Shhh...shhh...guys! Do you hear that?" Emily whispered. The girls fell silent.

Footsteps on the stairs grew louder. Taylor commanded the girls to move into the far corner of the attic behind a cobwebbed wardrobe. Emily and Sophie, who were as close as twins, clutched each other and trembled. When the footsteps stopped, all eyes were fixed upon the turning doorknob. The girls held their breath as the door slowly creaked open. They let out a sigh of relief as Aunt Carol appeared at the door and stepped through the doorway, locking it behind her. Frantic, Aunt Carol hurried the girls out an attic window to the roof. They were greeted by a loud rumbling noise, followed by the arrival of a shiny black helicopter with a dangling chair lift. As the girls each got lifted from the roof and seated in the helicopter, they admired the view below of the thick snow, now scattered with the occasional body of a knocked-out deliveryman.

Lindsey questioned, "Wait, what's going on?"

"What about our snowmen and cookies?" Sophie insisted.

"And our surprise package," whimpered Emily, who was shaking and clinging tightly to Sophie.

Taylor shouted, "Does it matter? We're going somewhere in a helicopter!"

"No time for questions; it's going to be fine," Aunt Carol reassured them. "I will explain everything later."

CHAPTER ONE

Mission Accepted

Emily snorted. "Wow, looking back at that day seven years ago, I cannot believe we thought those delivery men at Aunt Carol's house were real and not just pesky ACC members."

Sophie burst out laughing. "Ha! The Animal Cruelty Club (the ACC) always seems to find a way to locate us, except when we're at this Miniworld cabin headquarters. It's easy for us to find the ACC, because we're the only ones who can see their true form," she added.

"Exactly," nodded Emily. "It's our duty as the leaders of Miniworld to make sure that all animals have the best lives that they can."

"I still can't understand. Why does the ACC want to harm animals? Simply for their greedy purposes?" questioned Lindsey.

"Obviously, it's because all ACC members are heartless monsters and only interested in themselves," snapped Taylor as she rolled her eyes. Taylor often had a short fuse whenever anyone talked about mistreating animals. She became surrounded by large red bubbles that released steam as they popped. She became angrier. Pop, pop, pop, was all they heard as her bubbles increased in size.

"We get it, Taylor. Calm down," cautioned Emily. "Save your powers for our next run in with the ACC."

"Hey girls," interrupted Aunt Carol. "Could you come inside for a minute? I have your next mission to discuss."

Aunt Carol had designed this cabin to be disguised as a tiny winter ski lodge, but inside there was an enormous command post filled with all of the technology—plus a little "magic"—needed to complete their mission of defeating the ACC.

"What are we doing?" Lindsey replied.

"We're going on another adventure!" Taylor yelled over her shoulder as she ran toward the cabin. As she pushed the heavy door aside and waited for the others to catch up, she remembered the first time they'd seen the inside of the Miniworld headquarters.

"Do you remember the first time we saw this place?" asked Taylor.

"Yeah, it reminded us of Santa's workshop, with people and animals buzzing all around," added Emily.

"It seemed at least ten times bigger to us back then," Sophie recalled.

"Over here!" waved Aunt Carol from the back corner of the huge control room.

They hurried toward her as they struggled to keep their balance on the slick, freshly waxed floor. Inside, the scent of lemon cleaner mixed with the heat from the operating electronics greeted us. The room was filled with whirring and buzzing computers, spitting out information and displaying the latest information about the animal abuses happening across the world. When we reached the display, Aunt Carol pointed to a big headline running continuously across the screen, "Dolphin Slaughter Scheduled to Take Place in Japan Next Week."

"That sounds horrible!" screamed Emily.

"What is this dolphin slaughter thing?" wondered Lindsey.

"I don't know what it is exactly, but I know that I don't like it ONE bit!" shouted Taylor as a steaming red bubble formed around her and began lifting her up.

Emily reached up and popped the bubble as Taylor landed back on her feet.

Carol began to explain the details of the dolphin slaughter to the girls. They sat with eyes fixed on her, listening carefully to every word. As Carol continued to talk, she noticed the temperature around Sophie began to drop rapidly, and Emily's fingernails began to quickly grow longer and sharper. Lindsey grew a few inches taller as her feet started to rise off the floor.

"You have been practicing using your weapons and transforming from human to animal form for years now. So I know you're ready for this challenge," assured Aunt Carol.

She continued, "I understand that you are very upset to hear about this. But you need to pull it together and reserve your powers for your new mission to save the dolphins in Japan. Group hug!" Aunt Carol called out. She wrapped her arms around all of them in a loving embrace.

"Umm . . . I'm a little claustrophobic in here," Lindsey snarled politely, and everyone had a good laugh.

CHAPTER TWO

An Unexpected Visitor or Two

"Can I grab a snack?" Sophie asked her friends as they were running through the airport, frantically trying to find Gate C23 before their intended plane left to make the flight to Osaka, Japan. Sophie was gazing through the convenience store window as she crashed into a map of the airport. She was helped up by Frank the pug, who was their constant travel companion (along with Nelly the mouse).

"I have snacks packed in my carry on, Sophie. We only have eight minutes to find where we are going, and it's very confusing in here," Taylor responded.

"Wait, how long do we have to board the plane?" Lindsey questioned.

"Barely enough time," answered Emily.

They approached the gate just in time to see the flight attendant grab the microphone and announce, "Flight 1056 is now preparing for take off, and the gate is closing."

Taylor was quick to yell, "Hold on—we got four more on the way!" The flight attendant scanned their tickets and told them that their seats were in the back of the plane.

Lindsey was struggling to keep her breakfast down as her claustrophobia kicked in. The lack of legroom wasn't helping anyone to feel comfortable, but the girls offered Lindsey the window seat so she could peek out and see the world under her.

A few hours into the flight, the girls overheard the elderly woman seated in front of them, who had been knitting, discussing the dolphin drive with a fellow passenger. "I wish I had enough money to buy my granddaughter her own personal dolphin," she announced.

"Good luck with that!" replied the grumpy businessman seated next to her. "I heard that this year they were selling them for $200,000 each."

Taylor, unable to contain her anger any longer, leaned over the seatback and informed them, "As much fun as that idea sounds, you would be supporting the murder of thousands of intelligent marine mammals! Thousands more are taken from their habitat and forced into captivity for marine parks across the world. Those that aren't selected are slaughtered. Some of those that are killed become food that is toxic because of high levels of mercury. Now do you still want that dolphin?"

"If people have the money for it, they should be able to buy whatever they want," the lady bickered.

Taylor was fuming, and her voice got louder. "Don't you value the importance of marine life in our ecosystem? Or are you just as heartless as the dolphin slaughterers?"

The woman thought about this new information for a minute before snapping back, "Why don't you let the adults do the talking, young lady?" She whispered to the businessman, "Kids these days are so annoying and always trying to save the world even though it's fine at it is."

Frank let a low growl as Taylor slid back into her seat. As she gazed out the window, her thoughts turned to how hard this mission in Japan might actually be for them.

"Hush," whispered Lindsey, trying to calm Frank down.

"BOOM!" The plane began to shake, but the flight attendants calmed the passengers by saying that it was just a little wind. But the girls felt that something was not right. Lindsey used her amazing sense of smell to determine that the "wind" was actually the ACC trying to ruin the plans of saving the dolphins from the slaughter.

Sophie muttered to Frank, "I thought you said that the Animal Cruelty Club wasn't on our trail." She had made sure the other passengers on the plane could not hear her.

"I didn't think that they would find us either, Sophie," Frank said.

"Shhh!" Emily nudged Frank and looked around frantically, knowing that a talking dog, which was normal for them, would not go over well with the rest of the passengers.

They had thought earlier that they actually might get to Japan without the ACC holding them up, but now they were not too sure. Their worst fears were confirmed when Lindsey spotted the Mad Scientist's long, bony body suspended outside the window, his exposed brain glistening in the sunlight. He had a jet pack strapped to his back, and he had brought along a friend, a fisherman, perhaps the leader of the dolphin drive.

The Mad Scientist tightly grasped two test tubes. He was always using animal parts such as hair and blood to create a new concoction.

Beep . . . Beep . . . Beep . . .

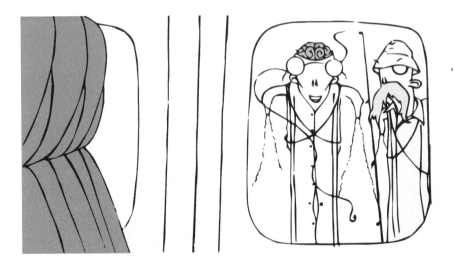

The noise of the Mad Scientist's jet pack failing filled the air.

"I'm running low on jet fuel," he whined. "I need to get in the plane," he snorted urgently in his obnoxious, nasally voice.

He took a test tube filled with a gooey green substance and threw the concoction on the window of the plane.

Sizzzzzzzzle.

The bubbly liquid began to eat through the window, and fast!

"A-ha, my solutions never fail me," the Mad Scientist smirked. He started to crawl through the opening in the window. The other ACC member quickly followed.

"Oh, my! Heavens to Betsy!" the old lady yelled, as the ACC climbed in through the hole in the plane.

"Time to morph," Taylor ordered.

"No," protested Frank. "There's too many passengers. You will blow our cover. I'm just sayin'." At his wise but nervous words, Taylor, Emily, Lindsey, and Sophie nodded seriously.

"Then we have to jump out of the plane," Sophie reasoned. "The ACC won't have enough fuel in their jet packs to follow us."

Lindsey nodded. "Frank is right," she said. "The people on this plane have seen way too much. We have to think about our cover."

Taylor remembered something important and offered, "When we were at Mini-world headquarters, our Fairy Godmother Aunt Carol and our staff artist, Bobbi LeBonte, gave me Anti-Memory Dust to help erase any unwanted memories."

"Awesome," Emily said. "Have you used it up yet?

"Nope," Taylor smiled. "I have it all right here in a little pouch."

Nelly the Mouse squeaked, "Get your parachutes out. Taylor, sprinkle the dust!"

Taylor wiped the memories from the passengers with the Anti-Memory Dust by taking small pinches from her cupped hand and sprinkling it above their heads. Seconds later everyone seemed dazed, but Taylor knew they didn't have long before the dust wore off and then their cover would really be blown, because they had transformed into their powerful animal forms.

"You girls are dreaming if you think you can stop the dolphin drive. We've been doing it for years," chucked the ACC fisherman with evil confidence in the ACC's plans.

"Yeah, what he said," the Mad Scientist agreed stupidly. His brains poked out of his head, and this problem seemed to have affected his intelligence. Nelly scurried along the overhead compartment and pounced onto the Mad Scientist's head, spraying lavender perfume in his eyes while Sophie and Emily closed in on him. Emily and Sophie had the ability to annoy the enemy into a state of severe confusion.

"C'mon," Sophie snickered. "We've got to hurry before they're able to walk again." She was impressed by her ability to annoy and confuse the ACC.

"This won't be the last of us . . . I assure you!" the Mad Scientist threatened through his clenched jaws.

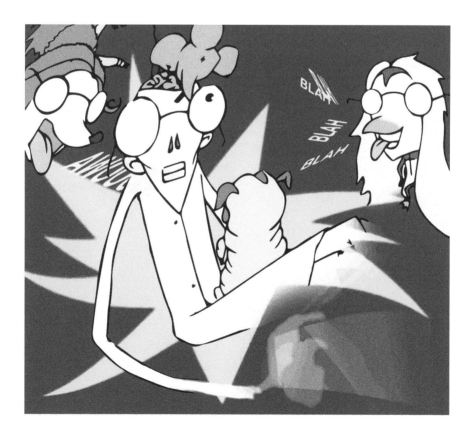

CHAPTER THREE

A Dumpling Encounter: Little Trouble in Big Osaka

As told by Emily

As soon as I landed, I quickly turned in a circle and scanned my surroundings. All I could see was the glimmer the sun had created on the ocean surface. I took a minute to admire the beauty around me and just floated in the water. After the rush of jumping out of the plane, all I can remember is landing here—but I'm not sure where "here" is! I was hoping that Taylor had a clue (because Taylor usually does). So I yelled for the girls.

"Lindsey, Sophie, Taylor!" I called. "Where are you guys?"

"Wait, where are we?" Lindsey asked.

The three of us responded simultaneously, "I don't know."

Sophie was hungry and just wouldn't stop complaining about food. I hoped I wouldn't have to hear much more of that. We decided it was time to get out of the water and swim to the closest island.

After a long swim to shore, we were relieved to be on land.

Sophie said, "Can we go get fast food?"

Taylor piped up in disgust, squinting at Sophie, "We are in the middle of the ocean, near Japan, on a deserted island, after we had to jump out of a plane, with the ACC right on our backs. And you are hungry? For fast food?"

"Yes!" Sophie screamed, her eyes bulging. Fast food had never sounded better to her.

"I am going for a swim," Taylor replied cheerfully. "I will see if I can signal any near-by dolphins." She did a double-back handspring into the ocean, and transformed into her dolphin form, her tail splashing water all over Lindsey.

"Where is Taylor going?" Lindsey asked, rubbing her head in confusion.

I zipped open my backpack in search of food. I found some apple juice, and some leftover waffles from Aunt Carol, our Fairy Godmother. We all know Aunt Carol is not the best cook, but she can sure make awesome waffles! Unfortunately the waffles were ruined by the salt water.

"Food!" Sophie exclaimed.

Within seconds, Sophie had eaten all of the waffles and never seemed to notice their normal crunch had been replaced with a soggy and salted taste.

"Guys, come on," Lindsey said, a bit too late as usual. "You two forgot to give me anything."

Finally, Taylor came back from her invigorating swim, and with her were a pod of bottlenose dolphins. She transformed back into her human form.

Sophie asked hopefully, "Now we can go get fast food?"

Taylor threw back her hair, rolled her eyes, and said, "No way."

Sophie sarcastically snipped, "Can I at least get a slushy?"

Their little squabble made me realize why we were here: not to bicker, but to help beautiful dolphins from being killed in the dolphin slaughter.

"We had better move quickly," Frank barked. "I smell the wretched ACC. Woof, woof."

"Put on your bathing suits," Taylor advised us.

Lindsey changed into a frilly pink bathing suit, which showed off her unique style. She batted her long eyelashes and cooed, "Is this cute?"

I took a picture of her to upload to her Instagram because we like to keep our followers engaged with our missions.

"Let's go!" Taylor rounded us up, smiling. "Time to go to the mainland!" Her eyes started to glow with anticipation of a job to do.

"Yay!" Sophie yelled as she waved her useless little wings and dove into the water. We followed her; yet Lindsey shied away.

We all grabbed onto a dolphin. I looked into the dolphin's eye and whispered, "We really will try our best to fix what's going on here." I helped Lindsey get on her dolphin, because she struggled. When you're a petite girl, nothing is easy. But we all help each other.

In no time at all, the little island where we had landed was a speck on the horizon.

When we got to the mainland, the dolphins let us off gently into the water, and we swam a few feet to shore. Then we landed on the beach, grateful to see land again.

"This is Osaka, known as the City of Water," Taylor announced, reading the big sign in the distance that told us of our location.

"Let's sit down for a while," Lindsey suggested.

"Yes," laughed Taylor. "We can start our tans."

So we rested on the beach and lathered on sunblock. But Taylor refused the lotion and continued to soak up the sun. At that point Frank ran, face first, into the water, to cool off his hot mug.

We discussed where to eat. Everyone ignored Sophie's requests for fast food, and we selected a fabulous veggie restaurant instead. Taylor phoned Kyuoko, a nearby restaurant, and made reservations. We walked up from the burning white sand to the bright-green pine trees. Next to the trees there was a large parking lot and a sign for the shuttle service. A yellow bus appeared, and we boarded paying the bus driver with Japanese Yen that Aunt Carol packed in our backpacks back in Miniworld headquarters.

"Yaho," the friendly bus driver greeted us. I knew that Yaho was a way of saying "hello" specific to Osaka. Our mentor back in headquarters, Victoria, had taught us simple Japanese phrases that might come in handy during our trip.

The drive took us down crowded streets with colorful advertisements and neon lights flashing in store windows. People bustled by, walking, in cars, or on bicycles. "There sure are a lot of people here," said Lindsey, in awe.

"You can say that again," I said.

"There sure are a lot of people here," Lindsey said.

"There are almost three million people in the city of Osaka," Taylor schooled us.

Sophie added, "Can you imagine how much food it takes to feed everyone? It makes me hungry to think about it. I can't wait to see the food go by on the restaurant's conveyor belt."

"I can't wait to ride on it," Sophie and I said at the same time. We got off the bus and ran toward Kyuoko, our mouths watering in anticipation.

We walked in and saw many people enjoying their meals, talking happily. Taylor walked up to the hostess with no hesitation and informed her of our arrival. We headed for the table, with chopsticks in hand. At the table, the waitress poured cups of green tea for us. As the rotating conveyor belt swung by our table, presenting food on brightly colored plates, we took which foods we wanted.

Never was food eaten with such relish and enthusiasm, as our starved group chowed down. I was the first to finish, so I jumped on the conveyor belt for a ride, balancing in a yoga position. I rotated gleefully on the belt next to a plate of shrimp with avocado and wasabi.

I glanced out the window and my eye was caught by two ACC fishermen in bright yellow trench coats and bucket hats. I looked a little harder, and their typical features shifted into a monstrous grin.

"Miniworld gang," I announced. "We have friends in the window," I warned as the ACC agents strolled in casually.

"We can't expose these people to our powers! We have to get them out of here!" Lindsey said, stressed.

"I am on it!" Taylor said as she slyly dashed across the room. I had no idea what she had up her sleeve until I heard sirens and I was soaked in water. With the fire alarm buzzing, diners made a stampede for the door in complete pandemonium. The restaurant was cleared out, and we ran into the kitchen so nobody would see our battle take place.

"Really Tay? That was your big plan! I straightened my hair this morning!" Lindsey complained as she whacked a fisherman around with her nunchucks.

Taylor was angered by their audacity to ruin our lunch date, feelings that made her bubbles spit out of her gun. She trapped the agent in a bubble, lifting him into the sky. Sophie and Emily had confused the other agent into a state of temporary paralysis that allowed Taylor the perfect opportunity to shoot one last bubble. The second agent began to float up.

Frank hadn't been talking much, and I had started to get worried about how he was acting. So I asked him, "Are you okay, Frank?"

"Ya, I just haven't felt right since we landed," he said.

"Like something's missing, but nothing's missing," I said as I looked around. It finally occurred to me, as well as everyone else, by the grim look on everyone's faces: Nelly the Mouse was gone! When had this happened, and where was she?

For the first time ever, we heard Frank whimper as he shrunk down and became silent. Frank had never been long apart from his best friend, Nelly the Mouse. Where was she?

CHAPTER FOUR

Unexpected Discovery

Everyone paced the hard wooden ground, brainstorming where Nelly might have disappeared.

"She could have found a cute guy mouse," Emily said, in a tone as hopeful as possible.

"Yeah," agreed Sophie. "As we speak, he might be taking her on a romantic walk on a famous Osaka beach."

"Who saw her last?" asked Taylor, always the one to get down to the forensic facts.

"I think I did," Frank piped up. "I saw her on the plane as we were fighting the ACC."

"So," Lindsey assumed, "when Nelly was fighting, the ACC must have grabbed her right before we jumped off."

"She's small enough that some ACC agent could have just scooped her up and stuffed her in his pocket," Taylor offered, her eyes narrowing.

"But why would they have done that?" Lindsey questioned.

"They were probably trying to distract us from our mission," stated Sophie.

"Well, in that case," growled Frank with intensity, "during the fight, one of them dropped a business card with the ACC's current location in Japan. I tucked it in my collar in case it could be important later. Maybe we could check there first?"

"Wow!" the girls said in unison, looking at the card. "Good thing you saved that!" Emily thanked him. Frank smiled puggishly.

Everyone locked arms and went skipping down the road. Soon they came to a nondescript building with a plain door. It looked ordinary, except for a sign that said in tiny print, "Tazei ni buzei."

"Few against many," Frank translated. "That certainly sounds like the ACC." Sophie had the courage to open the door. There was no one inside the long hallway. At the end of the hall, there was a right turn and a left turn.

"Let's split up," said Emily, leading Sophie to the left. Meanwhile, Taylor, Lindsey, and Frank went to the right.

As Emily and Sophie walked forward to the left, they noticed a hallway door slightly ajar. They peeked in and saw dozens of cages holding spoon billed sandpipers. They had heard that the ACC was harvesting the rare birds to use their bills as tea stirrers. The girls quickly went around opening up all the cages, and they ushered the sandpipers down the hall and out the front door. Immediately, the flock returned to the air and escaped, free at last!

During this time, Taylor and Lindsey had followed Frank to the right down the hallway. Frank followed his nose, and they ended up at the opening of the walk-in coat closet, where they made two more disturbing discoveries.

Lindsey slowly turned the cold doorknob and opened the creaking closet door. Expecting to smell mothballs and musty mold, she was surprised when she was greeted by the scent of lavender. That familiar smell reminded her of Nelly, who never left home without her lavender perfume, and the memory brought tears to Lindsey's big brown eyes. A muffled squeak came out of one of the dusty ACC lab coats hanging side by side, which was music to Lindsey's ears. She frantically tore the coats off the hangers in search of the missing Nelly. Deep in the pocket of one of the lab coats was a terrified and shivering little mouse—Nelly! She was so relieved to be reunited with her friends that she hopped right into Lindsey's backpack. It was only then that they all noticed a smelly ACC agent asleep in the back of the closet.

Frank gave the agent a little nip on the shoulder, waking him up. They forced him over to a small chair and tied him up to interrogate him.

"So what are you doing back here?" Taylor asked, but there was no answer from him. She could see that his name badge said "Victor Villiny."

"Villiny," she said, "we must have a serious talk."

"How did you find me in here?" Villiny asked.

Taylor smiled, "I don't know what it is about you ACC agents," she replied.

Lindsey added, "We see right through your human disguises to your real, monstrous identity."

Villiny asked, "So you thought it was a good idea to tie me to this chair?"

"Yes," Taylor nodded. "I want to find out from you what ACC knows about the dolphin slaughter."

"We know how it happens," he said with a sneer. "That's all I am allowed to say."

"How is the ACC involved?" Taylor asked.

"We're not," Villiny lied.

"Do you know who is killing the dolphins?" Lindsey said, pointing a finger at him.

"Yes. That is all I can say," he said, shrugging his shoulders.

"Do you know where it will happen, and when?" she asked, glaring at him.

"Yes. That is all I can say," he repeated smugly.

Taylor began dialing on her cell phone. "Fine," she said. "I'll have to leave you with the Ultra Twins. That is all I can say!" She smiled sweetly and was met with a cold silence from Villiny. "Ultra Twins, come on in," she said into the phone.

"Okay!" Villiny exclaimed suddenly. "I will tell you everything I know. Anyone but the Ultra Twins, those terribly irritating girls!" He was becoming terrified at the thought of having another run in with the Ultra Twins after having fought them on the plane.

He sighed heavily, and the truth came spewing out. "Many dolphins are captured at Tomo, although they are hunted other places, too. Many are killed for food, mostly sold in rural areas where dolphin has been a customary food for centuries."

Lindsey then asked, "I heard that food from dolphins is poisonous to people. Is that true?"

"Water pollution," he explained. "There's a high mercury level in bottlenose dolphins, so no one can eat a lot of it. Studies show that the Tomo people have more mercury in their systems than normal, but otherwise the people seem healthy."

Taylor then asked if all the captured dolphins were killed for food.

"No," he answered. "A few dolphins are not killed, but rather sold for high prices to businesses around the world, to entertain people."

"Go on," Nelly squeaked. "When will this take place?"

"The next time it will happen in Tomo is next week," he revealed.

Taylor was mad about the killing of the dolphins. She could have lost her cool.

She could have shot steam out of her ears. Her eyes could have bugged out of her head in her angry disbelief at his uncaring attitude. She could have called him a no-good, thoughtless, ACC nitwit. She could have whined about him endlessly, but Taylor decided to remain calm. Instead she did not call him any names. She thought hard about all the facts she knew about why dolphins should be considered too smart to be used for food.

Even if they were hunted for food in the past, science now has studied dolphins enough to know that dolphins are not just any fish. Researchers have studied the brains of dolphins and have made startling discoveries. She wanted to explain these findings to Villiny to change his mind, like she had tried to do with the woman on the plane.

Villiny replied, "I know all this, what is your point?"

"Well, let me tell you something you might not know," Taylor said. "Dolphins are beautiful. Plus their brain size, compared to their body size, is second only to the human brain. Bigger even than chimpanzees!" She motioned widely with her arms. "Their brains have many folds, which shows they're smart. Because they are intelligent beings, it's not ethical to hurt them, kill them for food, or keep them captive in parks for our amusement. Dolphins probably are even smarter than you or any other ACC agent."

She pointed directly at him. "How can you be part of this?" she protested.

"We're evil," he replied. "It's what we do."

"I don't believe that," Lindsey said, patting his shoulder. "Everyone can change.

You've just been evil so long, that you don't remember there is kindness in your heart."

He shook off her touch. "Okay, you've got your answers," he sneered. "Now cut me loose!"

Taylor, Lindsey, and Frank bolted for the door, and Lindsey tripped over a road sign and cones. Lindsey turned briefly to Villiny and said, "Buh-bye!"

Walking down the hallway, they spotted the Ultra Twins who shouted, "We'll explain everything later, let's get out of here—we found out that there are more ACC agents on the way!"

The girls rushed out of the building and grabbed a taxi to the hotel where they had reservations for the night.

The huge hotel had over four hundred rooms, but there was a catch. The rooms were very small and looked like large plastic tubes. Only one person could fit in each tube.

Emily complained in her capsule. "It's so small I can only lie down or sit up!"
Taylor added, "This is so uncomfortable."

Lindsey piped up, "Is this a tanning bed or a hotel? What's going on? I just busted a nail, and my eyelashes are brushing the ceiling whenever I blink."

The conversation was interrupted by Sophie's loud snore, who apparently didn't mind the close quarters.

CHAPTER FIVE

Reunited: To Tomo on the Road of Terror

As told by Sophie

For breakfast, I scarfed down three doughnuts, a big glass of orange juice, and a chocolate bar and was still hungry. We were shocked to see a van with the Miniworld logo on it pull up outside, and we guessed this was our ride. The passenger door opened, and I was greeted by a smiling Bobbi LeBonte! To meet us in Osaka, he had traveled all the way from our clubhouse headquarters in the United States. We were now going to drive from Osaka to Tomo where the dolphin drive is held.

Bobbi was dressed in black combat boots, but had left them untied. He wore skinny, black jeans, a jersey with red-striped sleeves, and a red baseball cap backwards over his brown hair. Set in his earlobes were round, large, gold earrings.

"Wow, we were not expecting you," Sophie greeted Bobbi.

"So what am I, ch-chop-chopped liver?" he wise cracked in his normal stutter. We laughed. He smiled at us between his oversized mustache and soul patch (which is a bearded spot right under his lower lip).

"We are glad to see you," Taylor said, poking me in the ribs.

"Yes, we are," I quickly agreed. "But we are confused."

"I know!" Bobbi grinned. He explained, "Your f-f-f-airy Godmother, Carol, sent me here."

Between the front seats was his big, black sketchbook. When he opened it up, I saw that he had made many large drawings of dolphins.

"I admire how d-d-different sea life is from us," Bobbi said happily.

"I think it's amazing that they don't use words to communicate, but use sounds like whistles and clicks, which are like words to them. Some of the sounds they make are so high that we can't even hear them. They can even make a noise on two different notes at the same time," explained Sophie.

Taylor observed, "Those are neat drawings that you did of the dolphins talking to each other."

"Thanks! In this drawing," Bobbi said, "the dolphins are ca-call-calling each other by name."

I finally managed to get back into the conversation after being ignored, saying, "When one dolphin is looking for the other in the dark sea, she calls out the whistle name of the dolphin she is trying to find. When the friend hears his name, he swims over."

"Cool," said Emily, trying to mimic the dolphin sound by making a buzzing and clicking noise.

"Also," I continued, "dolphins have a type of sonar that is even better than we have invented. With their sonar, they can pinpoint exactly the distance and size of any nearby object."

Lindsey wondered out loud, "I think that's called photosynthesis...or maybe echolocation?"

Emily jumped in saying, "Photosynthesis is how plants make their own food, and echolocation is when animals use sound waves in order to communicate and judge distance."

Taylor said, "I can already understand dolphin. We want to have a conference with some of the dolphins outside of Tomo, where the hunt is."

"That's exactly what I th-th-thought you would do," Bobbi said. "So I brought a waterproof crittercam that you can use. It sends a television image and audio voice to a screen in the v-v-van. The cam has the capability of translating dolphin sounds into any language, with a d-d-device newly developed by a scientist, Dr. Mishimi, in T-T-Tokyo. I can-can drive you to Tomo so that you will be there by late afternoon. Then you can take a moonlight swim with the d-d-dolphins out to sea to have the conference."

"We will have to move quickly," said Lindsey. "The hunt starts tomorrow. We need to stop it from happening!"

"Yes, let's leave today," Emily said. "I don't want to sleep in a tiny capsule again tonight anyway."

We hopped in the van and headed to Tomo, taking the fastest route along the green mountain hillsides. Along the way, we told Bobbi all about what the ACC had been up to. Bobbi belted out the latest hit songs, and we sang along.

We were so busy singing, that we failed to realize the impending danger ahead: a roadblock. Bobbi stomped on the brake, causing the back wheels to skid along the cement road. As we tried to stop, the van swerved, and the vehicle began to slip over the edge of the road. Terrified, I saw that the other side of the road plummeted down the mountain at least thirty feet.

"Quick," Bobbi said. "Everyone lean hard to the l-l-le-left!"

We leaned to the left inside the van, but the van still teetered on the very edge. Nelly clung to the right side of the steering wheel.

"You, too, Nelly!"

When she moved, the van regained its balance, and Bobbi quickly pushed a button on the dashboard. Wings popped out of the side of the van, and WHOOOSH, he flew the vehicle right over the roadblock.

Frank wiped sweat off his furrowed brow. "I thought it was the end! My whole life flashed before my eyes, back to when I was a puppy."

"Boy, that was close!" Emily agreed, taking a big breath.

"You can say that again!" I exclaimed, still terrified.

"But I won't," laughed Emily.

As we flew over, we examined the roadblock carefully.

"Don't you think it's kind of strange that this sign is written in English?" Taylor questioned.

"I agree, quite fishy!" I responded.

"It smells of that pesky ACC critter I met back in Osaka, named Villiny," Taylor advised everyone.

Bobbi wondered out loud, "How c-c-could the ACC have known you were coming down this road today?"

"Well," Taylor surmised, "they're lacking a few brain cells, but sometimes they get it right." We continued on our way.

The group sat silently as we calmed ourselves down after our near-death accident.

Emily broke the silence, "Why do so many Tomo people agree with the dolphin slaughter?"

"It is b-be-because their ancestors have always hunted the oceans," Bobbi answered. "It is hard to break with the p-p-past traditions. But today, scientists are able to prove that dolphins are smart and should not be used for food."

"The people probably think that we, as outsiders, are interfering with their customs," Taylor offered.

"But we mean no disrespect to the town," Emily said. "Our country also has many problems."

"It is hard to break with the past," nodded Lindsey.

Frank offered a "woof" in agreement.

Everyone went silent again as we rode along. We knew that what was ahead of us could be dangerous. In the village would be the townspeople, the hunters, police, the ACC, the dolphins, and the activist protesters. It was a sure bet that things would not go smoothly.

CHAPTER SIX

Love Is in the Air: Buzz Off!

In late afternoon, Bobbi announced that they were approaching Tomo. They had driven onto a little peninsula of land, and houses were packed between steep hills. The dark-green mountains contrasted sharply with the deep-blue sea.

They parked near some trees by the beach and noticed a Tomo teenager sitting on the shore. When he heard Bobbi and the girls approach, he turned, chuckling, shaking his straight, raven hair.

"Hello," he said. "Welcome to my village."

"Hi," said Taylor. "You speak good English."

"That's nice of you to say," he said. "My mom taught me. She lived in Australia. I am planning someday to visit the United States."

"You will like our country," Emily said. "This is our first time in Japan. Your town is in a pretty place."

The Japanese boy introduced himself as Taro Tanaka. The girls introduced themselves and said that they were there to save the dolphins and that they go on animal rights missions as part of their Miniworld team.

"There are many fun things to do in Japan," Taro said, "You'll definitely have a good time while you're here."

"I guess so," said Emily.

"Yeah," Taro replied. "You will probably be interested to hear that my father is a hunter. Only the best hunters are chosen, by a ritual. The hunt starts tomorrow, and it is very important income to our town. It brings in money, from aquariums, to the people he works for."

"I see," said Taylor, wondering why anyone would kill dolphins. She gulped hard, nervous that Taro's father was a hunter. She hoped she didn't sound like a tourist to the boy when she asked, "Do many people eat dolphin?"

"Not anymore," said Taro, shaking his head. "It has mercury. Most people eat other fish. I don't eat it." He rubbed his nose to make Taylor laugh. "I think it smells bad," he chuckled.

Taylor was suitably charmed. She decided he was probably about her age. Puzzled, she hoped Taro would explain more about why the townspeople needed to hunt dolphin.

Bobbi asked, "Is everyone in t-t-town involved in the dolphin hunt?"

"Yes," replied Taro. "The dolphin hunt is our town's best income source—along with getting dolphins for the aquariums."

"Why are dolphins killed?" Emily asked.

"When they choose dolphins for the aquariums, the unchosen ones are killed because the staff isn't large enough to keep all of them for a long time. Most of these are sold for pet food and fertilizer," explained Taro.

Lindsey noticed that when Taro said pet food, Frank started gagging in her backpack, imagining what could have been in the dog food he ate earlier.

Taro further explained, "In our culture, everyone must work. If the town isn't doing well, and there are no jobs, people would have to leave—like many kids are already doing when they've finished high school."

Bobbi pointed out, "People here don't have a lot of money. The l-la-land is too steep to farm."

Taro said, "Our paper mills are closed. Due to computers, there was not as much need for paper. But we know how to hunt marine life."

"Thank you for explaining this to us," said Lindsey.

"My pleasure," Taro said, but he was looking mainly at Taylor.

She batted her eyelashes back at him.

Taylor saw kindness in Taro, and that he was a lot like her. She liked him for who he was, friendly and honest. She had been realizing that this case wasn't as simple as she had originally thought. Never before had she considered the heritage of fishing and catching dolphin in the way that Taro had explained it. She hadn't realized before that the villagers had very few options for economic livelihood, and she now understood what the dolphin catch meant to them.

Her thoughts were cut short when she heard Emily scream and saw Bobbi LeB-onte suddenly hop up several feet into the air. All chaos had broken loose; it was pandemonium. A loud buzzing sound came at them from the forest. What looked like a small fighter squadron rushed out of the mountain trees and nose-dived right into their group.

Bobbi was now flailing his arms and running for the shelter of the van.

Bobbi had somehow made hundreds of hornets very angry. Only these hornets weren't normal-sized; rather they were huge, almost the entire length of a finger. In the nick of time, he managed to get inside the van and slammed the door shut behind him when one of the marauding divers crashed into the window.

Lindsey grabbed her nunchucks from the roof of the van and began forcing some of the gigantic, yellow-headed hornets back into the forest. Then she, too, retreated to the safety of the van.

Sophie ran to help, but Taro motioned her to get into the van.

"You're wearing some perfume!" he yelled to Sophie. "It attracts them, so get into the van."

"What are they?" Taylor asked Taro in horror. The two daring fighters were both using identical martial arts moves from side to side to keep one step ahead of the whirring, flying beasts.

"Suzumebachi," replied Taro as calmly as possible, as he continued to thwart the attackers. "Giant, relentless hornets."

Suddenly, Taylor cried, "Get off me, you creepy thing!" There was one crawling slowly but deliberately up her neck, which she was trying to brush off. Abruptly, she stiffened and said, "I got stung! Help!"

Taro rushed over to her, his dark eyes flashing, to find the hornet on her skin. "Buzz off!" he yelled and bravely swatted off the offending insect.

Taylor swooned into a faint and fell into his arms. He yelled to Emily, "Come quickly, and help me carry her to the van. Getting stung once isn't a problem, but getting stung twice means certain death!"

Together Emily and Taro carried Taylor to the van, and everyone stayed there for a while, watching the killer hornets surround them and climb on the outside of the windows. The tremendous sound of the humming rocked the van and did not let up.

Taylor awoke, very glad to be inside the van. She said that being stung had felt like a hot needle.

Taro explained to her that one sting would not be lethal, but that she would feel tired and sick to her stomach for a while.

Bobbi looked out the window at the hornets' big black eyes staring at them and said, "Geez, those are some n-nasty critters."

"Yes," agreed Taro. "They will chase you up to three miles and can easily outrun you. But if you think they're big, you should see our bears."

Bobbi started up the van, which caused the hornets to gradually loosen their grip on the vehicle. As he drove Taro home, one by one the hornets flew back to the trees. Fortunately, the giant insects did not follow, so Taro was able to get out of the van, turn and bow goodbye.

Taylor saw a curtain move at the window, probably Taro watching them drive away. She was hopeful that he liked her, but she felt upset that their ideas about the dolphins were so far apart.

The girls were anxious to go out to the ocean for a conference with the dolphins.

Bobbi drove them to the spot on the shore where they were meeting some of the dolphins to catch a ride out to sea. Frank and Nelly stayed behind in the van with Bobbi.

There was a slight breeze, and it had become a lovely night. Sometimes the clouds moved and revealed a glimpse of the moon. The sea came in to the shore in a bit of a rush, causing a low, crashing sound. The girls looked out to the water and saw two dolphins waiting for them. They grabbed the crittercam and waded out to the dolphins.

Taylor seemed to be feeling better from the hornet sting. Lindsey and Emily were holding tight to a dolphin.

Taylor and Sophie swam by their side in their animal forms. They dipped and glided through the waves, roaming far out to sea.

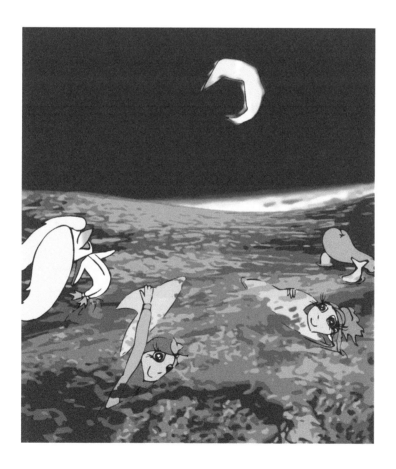

CHAPTER SEVEN

Meeting with the Dolphins

As told by Lindsey

We were traveling at night on the Kumano-nada sea. As we ventured farther out through the frigid waves, way past the Tomo shoreline, the wind whipped back my hair. Every now and then, the moon slipped through the clouds; but for the most part, the night was jet black. I smelled the strong scent of seaweed. Although the water was murky below me, I could hear the dolphins talking through the water, far up ahead.

"I'm so glad you know where you're going," I said to Taylor.

Emily, her mouth full of hair, said, "Yuk! And it's salty, too! I'm cold."

Ahead a few yards, I saw a soft light, as if blue candles had been spread out under the water. I saw that many dolphins were there to greet us. Emily got out the crittercam, so that Bobbi in his van on the shore, could hear the dolphins speaking and see the meeting.

"I am Chiyo," said one of the dolphins. "We hope you like our meeting spot in the blue sea sparkle. It is from algae. We like to play here each night."

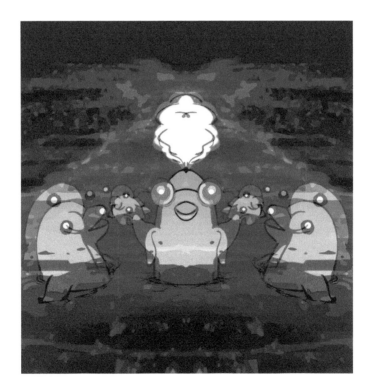

Sophie splashed at the blue sea sparkle with her little penguin wings, and a turquoise flash of ocean spray jumped up into the sky.

"Awesome!" said the Ultra Twins.

"Amidst all this beauty, we come here with serious news," Taylor said to the dolphins.

"Open your hearts to us," said Chiyo, as the other dolphins nodded.

"The dolphin drive starts tomorrow in Tomo Cove. You must warn as many dolphins as you can to stay away," I said.

"We knew it would start soon," Chiyo said, sadly. "We have made preparations to get the word out to our families. But nearby boats are using sonar that interferes with our messages in the water."

Another dolphin moved forward to speak. "I am Katsu, Warrior of the Deep. We wanted to tell you something, too."

We listened closely to her.

"There is a forgotten thing in the Cove," she continued.

"What is it?" asked Taylor.

"We don't know what it is," Katsu said, "because most dolphins who go that far into the Cove are killed or taken far away. We have heard rumors, from some dolphins who have escaped, that something dangerous lies nestled in the rocks at the bottom of the Cove. We know that it can hurt the whole village."

"What should we do?" Sophie asked. "The ACC will be there tomorrow. Protesters and police will be all over the beach. Bobbi will be in a van in the parking lot, and Mr. Tanaka, one of the hunters, will be in the Cove to capture dolphins. He is the father of Taro, our friend."

Taylor quickly sucked in her breath a little, and I could tell that perhaps she was thinking of Taro as more than just a friend.

Emily said, "We not only have to stop the dolphins from being killed, but we have to keep danger away from all of those people in the village."

"I have a plan," said Katsu, "if you are brave enough to do it."

"Yes!" we said in unison, eagerly.

"I will wear the crittercam and go into the Cove," said Katsu. "Taylor, you seem very outgoing, and I have seen that your animal form is a strong swimmer. Can you come with me to search for the forgotten thing?"

"Yes," Taylor said, her eyes shining a fierce blue, reflecting the water.

"Lindsey, I see you have nunchucks," Katsu observed. "We will need you to temporarily confuse the hunters with your special nunchuck moves."

I agreed.

Katsu went on, "Emily, I bet you can be very annoying." Emily smiled gleefully. "Then would you like to help Sophie frustrate the ACC to tears?"

"I certainly would," Emily replied.

"I have something you could use," Taylor said, handing Sophie and Emily each a package from her backpack. "It's too early for my birthday," said Emily.

"Is it Christmas already, and I forgot?" Sophie said, puzzled.

"When Frank and I went to the ACC building in Osaka," Taylor explained, "we ended up finding Nelly in a walk-in clothes closet. As we left, I picked up two ACC uniforms. You can wear them and infiltrate the ACC security."

"Oh, I just love dress-up missions," Sophie said, smiling.

"Sophie and I will go back to the beach," said Emily. "We will talk to Bobbi about setting up the crittercam TV and speaker so that all the Tomo people can see what the forgotten thing is."

"Bobbi also told me that he had another techno trick up his coat sleeve," I laughed. "I don't know what it is yet, but I'm certain it will do the trick!"

"Then it is done," Katsu said. "Taylor, Lindsey, and I will head to the Cove. Sophie and Emily will handle the beach."

"It will be a dangerous mission, but we will prevail. As a wise Japanese poet once said: 'Individually, we are only one drop in the sea. Together, we are a mighty ocean.'" said Chiyo solemnly.

All the dolphins whistled. We cheered. We all knew we had a dangerous job to do.

CHAPTER EIGHT

The Undersea Search Mission

As partially told by Taro

I tossed and turned in my bed under the full moon. It was the night before the dolphin drive and I felt restless, because I knew the next day that my father had to go out to help hunt the dolphins. I also could not stop thinking about the intelligent and beautiful girl I had recently met at the beach with some of her friends. I've never met anyone who inspired me to think twice about being empathetic toward animals. Her passion for animal rights was contagious, and I couldn't wait to see her again.

Her eyes had put me under her spell! I wanted to find out what she was up to, and after dinner I walked down to a spot near the shore where their van was parked. I was surprised to find out from Bobbi that Taylor had gone swimming in the cold ocean with her Miniworld friends.

Bobbi looked at me and nodded solemnly, saying, "Koi no yokan" with his American accent. I don't know how to translate that phrase into English, other than to admit that I was falling for her.

With skillful hands, he rigged up some complex electronics that beamed wirelessly to a phone, so that I could see the girls out in the ocean on the crittercam. I could hear them by a special speaker on the cam that translated dolphin into any language. He told me that they'd just had a big meeting with the dolphins, and that the dolphins had said there was a dangerous forgotten thing in the Cove. I knew I needed to tell my father, so I went back home with the phone that Bobbi had given me, where I could watch everything unfold on the device.

After Lindsey, Taylor, and a dolphin they called Katsu the Warrior left the evening's meeting out in the ocean, they must have shot like missiles through the black water to reach their target: the Cove. They were such strong young women. They needed to find the dangerous forgotten thing, and also they wanted to keep the dolphin drive from happening. I was amazed to see sweet Taylor in her dolphin form, carrying a bubble gun and Lindsey in her pig form with her nunchucks.

"We must hurry," I heard Lindsey say. "Soon the hunters will be here to capture the dolphins."

When they got to the Cove, it was still night, and there was a deadly silence, like the calm before a storm. They knew that many dolphins would die or be captured that day if they did not succeed.

I heard a knock on my bedroom door and my father entered the room.

"Father, you have to see this!" I exclaimed while handing him the phone. "This is the live feed of the dolphins in the Cove. The dolphins are trying to warn us about a forgotten thing in the Cove that could harm our village."

He raised his hand to his mouth in disbelief.

"I can't believe this is happening," he nodded. "This device is incredible! For years I've been listening to their buzzing and clicking, but I had no idea they were this smart!"

As I stared down at the device, I could see that Taylor quickly went looking for the forgotten thing in every nook and cranny of rock and sea floor that there was to explore.

The dolphin called Katsu, like all dolphins, had a natural ability to find things, called sonar. With sonar, dolphins can locate an object ahead. It did not matter that the water was dark and murky; Katsu could still look for the forgotten thing with her sonar ability. Even in the darkest water, she would be able to tell the size and shape of an object, and how far away it was. Taylor had said that a dolphin could even tell the difference between a quarter and a dime.

"Click, click!" Katsu made little noises, but my father and I could see that she did not find anything but rocks.

We watched them swim up and down the shore of the Cove, looking high and low within its shadowy depths.

"Click, click," Katsu repeated.

As they searched the rocky coast, Lindsey spoke up. "Perhaps the story of the forgotten thing is just a legend."

Katsu gave Lindsey a gentle, reassuring nudge and replied, "In Japan, we say nanakorobi yaoki, which means that perseverance is better than defeat. You might fail seven times, but succeed the eighth time."

My father and I were amazed to hear Katsu speak, and that a dolphin could be so wise. But we knew already, having lived near the ocean, that dolphins are extremely determined in their efforts to hunt, protect their young, and survive.

As told by unknown…

At the same time that Taro was watching the phone with his father, Sophie and Emily were climbing out of the black water and heading for the van. Once the girls were on the beach, they waved farewell to their dolphin rides and strode up through rocks and sand to greet Bobbi, who was parked at a spot near the Cove. He ran over to meet the girls.

"It's freezing," whined Emily.

Sophie replied, "Got you a towel, Em!"

"The crittercam and audio worked well," he said, smiling. "I saw the c-con-conference with the dolphins and was able to understand most of what they were saying! Come, rest for a while in the van."

He had some food ready for them and blankets, so that they could catch a few winks next to Frank and Nelly.

Emily sighed as she snuggled in the blanket, relaxing from the night's ride.

Everyone rested inside the van, lulled into sleep by the crashing of the waves.

Just prior to sunrise, when it was still dark, they woke up and saw Bobbi outside the van sketching the colorful horizon. In the van, Sophie and Emily quickly dressed up in the stolen ACC uniforms. Frank was so startled to see them this way that he gave a little bark.

"Frank," Sophie asked, "do you think we look evil enough?"

"Yep," he replied. "Most definitely bark-worthy."

They laughed, and they heard Nelly's high-pitched snicker as Bobbi came back into the van. The little mouse was peeking out of Bobbi's coat pocket. She nudged him in the ribs.

"Oh, yes," he said. "My bad, I am a mo-most forgetful artist! Nelly is reminding me that I have a few small helpers for you."

Emily said excitedly, "Let's see!" Something buzzed past her ear.

"Oh!" she cried out in surprise. "What in the world is that?"

Three tiny metal objects whizzed past again, too fast to be seen well in the van.

The three objects rested on Bobbi's head, so that the girls could get a good look.

"That's awesome!" exclaimed Sophie. "These are the robotic hummingbirds we designed back at Miniworld headquarters. They can translate any language."

Bobbi explained, "You're right. They are your remote-controlled robot drones. I can fl-fly them anywhere. Inside each is a m-miniature camera, s-so that they can show us the way. Further, their needle beaks pack quite a little punch. Very effective in getting someone to move qu-quickly. You girls spent so much time working on the prototypes before you left. I knew you would want to h-h-have them with you."

One hovered in front of Emily's face.

Emily said, "Between these little flapping dudes and our powers, I think that we can be up to 8.5 on the annoyance scale."

"Make that 9.5," Sophie said.

"Whatever!" Emily stuck out her tongue and laughed.

They smiled, downed some cold waffles that were left over, and stepped out of the van. A low-tide smelly ocean wind hit them in the face.

"Well, that was beautiful," Sophie observed sarcastically; and as her animal form, she did a few high flaps to warm up.

Emily studied Sophie's face. "What's your famous intuition on this one?" she

asked, watching the athletic Sophie, energized from a lot of high flaps, change back into her human form.

"Well," Sophie began, looking up and down at Emily's ACC outfit, "I think you look better in your soccer uniform, but I'm sure that the ACC will think you're one of them. Are you ready to be your annoying self?"

Emily shot back, "I have a few famous ACC impersonations up my sleeve."

As they approached the Cove, daylight was just beginning, yet the beach was already active. Protesters were beginning to gather, but they could only go so far. The police had set up a perimeter of barricades to keep the protesters back from the water. The ACC were up on the dock with microphones, trying to control the crowd of protesters in front of them, and trying to keep the protesters behind the barriers.

Far behind the ACC, out in the ocean, large white boats were lined up to channel the unwitting dolphins into the Cove. Smaller boats were edging the dolphins closer to the beach, using loud noise to move them along. The ACC agent in these boats soon would be moving the dolphins with nets, bringing killed dolphins into their boats, and moving others to enclosed pens near the shore.

Emily and Sophie could easily see what was happening out in the water and on the dock, because the drone hummingbirds were sending video back to their phones. The girls knew that some of the caught dolphins would be sold to aquariums. But many dolphins would be moved to other areas to be killed. The girls saw that these areas were covered by blue and green tarps. On the other side of the Cove, the hummingbirds showed the girls a building where the killed dolphins would be processed.

The ACC was providing security so that the protesters could not go out into the water and free the dolphins.

Sophie and Emily slouched up the boardwalk where the ACC were giving the public false information. Because the girls had on uniforms, they got past all the police barriers and went right up to where four ACC agents were standing at microphones, facing the public.

Sophie looked one straight in the eye and said, "We're the next shift, and we're replacing you."

"Nah," the ACC agent replied. "We still have an hour left."

"Plus," Emily added, "your wife called, and she says you have to go home to take the dog to the vet."

"That can't be so," he countered. "Why not?" Emily asked.

"Because I don't like animals," he explained. "I don't have any pets."

Emily turned to the gathering crowd. The drone hummingbirds translated for her as she said, "Keep that in mind. He's not an animal lover. He despises them."

The ACC agent was aghast. "What ACC department are you from, anyway? You are making me look foolish up here in front of everyone."

"Well, you have to admit," said Emily, "that you don't have much common sense. All the recent science studies show that dolphins are highly intelligent creatures, yet you're telling these people that dolphins are no smarter than chickens. In fact, I think most chickens are smarter than you."

"We don't read those studies," he said.

People in the audience roared with laughter at his excuse.

At that point, Sophie began showing the public all her best soccer tricks, which everyone found highly entertaining.

Everyone was now busy watching Sophie, and they did not see the humming-birds slowly poke the real ACC agents on the shoulder, buzzing around their heads, until the ACC got so dizzy that they fell off the dock to the beach below.

Emily hopped down off the boardwalk to follow them, changed into her hedgehog self, and sent several spines flying toward the backsides of the retreating ACC. They yelped and ran away even faster, pursued by their tormentors. Emily as a hedgehog was able to zip through the sand and rock much easier than the ACC agents, and she was close behind.

"YES!" Emily squealed with delight.

The ACC agents had been humiliated by being made to look stupid on stage by a couple of teenaged girls. They felt disgraced that they had to retreat from the constant buzzing, poking, stinging, and prodding from Emily's spine arrows and long, sharp beaks of the robots. They began to be annoyed to tears.

Even as the ACC agents were racing forward, the little hummingbirds hovered in front of their faces and collected the tears from their eyes. Even a few drops of ACC tears can be made into a mighty potion. When ACC tears are mixed with tears of laughter from one of the girls, such as laughing at one of Sophie's hilarious comebacks, the potion can make an ACC goon turn into a normal person again.

Now that the real ACC were running away, Sophie motioned to the protesters.

"Here!" she said, "You can get through the barriers at this point. Who wants to cut some nets?"

Three people raised their hands. One of Sophie's strengths is as a swimmer, and with robust strokes, she led them out into the cold water where the nets were. Hunters used the nets to move the dolphins. Sophie's group poked holes in the nets, and some of the dolphins were able to escape.

All of this time, no matter how busy Sophie and Emily were, they could not help but wonder how their buddies Taylor and Lindsey were doing on this chaotic but important day. They were about to find out.

CHAPTER NINE

The Undersea Search Mission

As told by Taro

Throughout the night, my father and I stayed glued to the phone, watching the brave girls and dolphins hunt for the forgotten thing. We saw that a few dolphins nearby had heard Taylor making clicking sounds and had come over.

"This is a dangerous place today," Taylor told the dolphins. "Hunters will be capturing and killing dolphins here. You must leave and warn any other dolphins nearby."

A dolphin from the group started nosing around the bottom of the ocean floor with Katsu. "What are you searching for?" he asked Katsu.

Katsu replied, "Hello, Daisuke. We heard a story that there is a dangerous forgotten thing hidden in the Cove. We must find it to keep the village safe."

Daisuke the Great Helper Dolphin said to the dolphin group, "Go to the entrance of the Cove, and warn other dolphins to stay away. I will remain here in the Cove, to help look for the forgotten thing."

My father and I saw dolphins rush to the front of the Cove to try to keep other dolphins from entering. We could see that dawn was beginning to break, and that big white boats from the village were preparing to come out to the ocean.

Suddenly, Katsu whistled. "What is that, up ahead?" she said, peering into the dark water. "It seems too long to be a rock. It almost looks like metal."

My father grew anxious about what it could be, and he peered carefully at the phone screen.

Daisuke said, "I agree. I'm approaching it now. Katsu, can you get the crittercam focused close-up on this thing?"

Katsu moved forward, carefully swimming so as not to touch the object. "Yes!" Katsu said, vigorously bobbing her head. "This must be it."

Taylor, hearing that Katsu had found the forgotten thing, pushed her way to the surface.

Lindsey followed. I could tell that Taylor wanted to get an idea of how close they were to the shore. She was thinking intelligently, something I find very intriguing. It was now dawn, and boats with hunters were spreading out around the Cove.

Without warning, a small metal hummingbird hovered in front of Taylor's face. "Hello there!" Lindsey said, seeing the hummer. "Who are you?"

To her amazement, the little hummingbird spoke in Bobbi's voice, saying, "This is Bobbi, talking to you through my n-new-newly invented flying drone. I can see you from the crittercam."

Bobbi instructed, "Katsu, get closer, we need to get a better look!"

Katsu grabbed the crittercam and dove to the bottom of the cove until she reached the glimmering metal of the forgotten thing.

As she inched closer, her tail skimmed the surface of the mystery object causing it to come loose from its perch between two rocks and skitter further down to the ocean floor.

"I think it's a piece of a ship," said Katsu.

"I think it's an oil tank," I commented.

"No, it looks more like a…" added my father.

"b-b-b-b-b-bo-BOMB!" screamed Bobbi.

We all held our breath as we observed the forgotten bomb sinking rapidly toward the rocky floor.

I've always done well in history at school, so I knew that old bombs can still explode after many years. This one could have been left here from a war a long time ago, then it was forgotten. It could blow up the whole village, and all the marine life in our area in a matter of minutes.

Bobbi frantically announced, "We need to call for help now to raise the bomb and defuse it."

Taylor took charge, gulped in fear, and then pushed that fear immediately away to her tail. "Okay," she said bravely, "Lindsey and I will go to the boats to get help raising the bomb. Katsu will stay here to pinpoint the bomb's location."

My father and I could hear the sound of our own breath, as we were frozen in shock. The sharp ring of the telephone sliced through the silence, causing us to jump. An anxious Bobbi wanted to talk to my father, and they agreed that my father would call the Tomo police right away to go out to the Cove and defuse the bomb.

I was watching Taylor both on the phone and from visuals I was receiving with the hummingbird drones. Of course, she knew that communicating to the hunters in the boats would not be an easy thing. What if the hunters harmed them accidentally? I was worried. As the girls approached the boats, I could see that the hunters had already herded some dolphins into a group. The hunters were using nets and loud noises to herd the dolphins into an area where the animals could be killed.

Taylor and Lindsey edged closer, knowing they must be careful, but also aware that they must move quickly to get help.

Lindsey and Taylor sliced through the cool water as they quickly made their way to the boat. The dolphins had stopped further out as they were keeping their distance from the dangerous nets. As Taylor raced forward, she noticed that Lindsey was now yards behind her.

"Help! Something is pulling at my hooves!" cried Lindsey.

When Taylor turned around, all she could see was Lindsey's head bobbing just above the waves. Despite Taylor's exceptional swimming ability, she wasn't fast enough to reach Lindsey before she was sucked violently under the water.

Taylor cried out, "She can't swim!" But all Taylor could see now was a little patch of bubbles appear on the top of the water. Lindsey was gone.

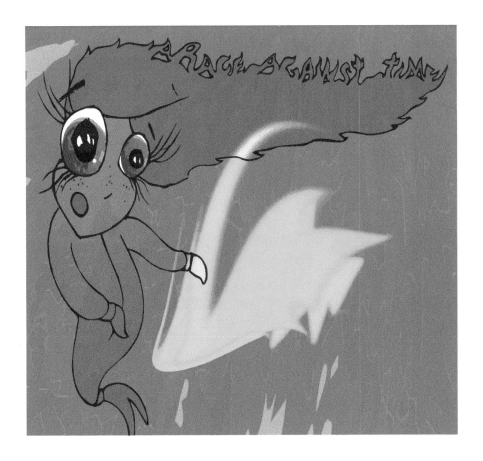

CHAPTER TEN

A Race Against Time

Soft white bubbles trickled to the surface of the ocean. Taylor watched the bubbles in horror, knowing she might never see her friend again.

"What's going on?" Lindsey cried, her head bobbing up over the waves for a breath of air, with her hoof stuck in what looked like a clump of seaweed. "You have got to be kidding me. Help Tay!"

Taylor could not hear her over the roar of the boat engines.

The next thing Lindsey knew was the feeling of being dragged out of the water and thrown to the slippery floor of the boat with a thud. The wind was knocked out of her, and she struggled to breathe. Surrounding her was a tight net. She could wiggle, but she could not get loose. All around the boat, she could hear dolphins in the water, whistling and crying, scared by the noise and trying to avoid the harpoons.

Above all this noise, Lindsey heard the distinct crackling of the boat's radio.

"Boat Two! Boat Two! Answer, please! This is Mr. Tanaka with a very important message from Bobbi!"

A big boot pressed against Lindsey's side. It was a hunter. Terrified, she looked right in his face. Thanks to one of Bobbi's overhead electronic translating humming-birds, she could understand the hunters in Japanese and respond likewise.

"If that isn't the weirdest looking dolphin I ever saw," said the hunter. He mo-tioned for another hunter to come over to that side of the boat. "What do you make of this, Han?"

"That's no dolphin," said Han. "Wait! That's a pig. What are you doing here, Wilbur?" He cut Lindsey (still in her animal form) loose. She instantly used her nunchucks to cause the dolphin hunters to lose their balance.

"Not one step farther!" she warned in Japanese. "And do not call me Wilbur."

"Have we been at sea too long, or are you actually talking?" the hunters asked Lindsey, shrugging. "What's your story? Aren't you a bit off the farm?" they laughed.

"No time for that now! The dolphins found a bomb left forgotten from World War II in the Cove," Lindsey explained quickly. "If it explodes, it will destroy the whole village. You must quickly take the boat to where the bomb is, to help move it out to sea."

The hunters scratched their heads, bewildered.

"How do we know this is the truth?" they said.

"Go to your radio," Lindsey advised, "because there is a message for you from Mr. Tanaka. He can explain best what has been going on."

"I saw the bomb," Mr. Tanaka exclaimed through the crackling radio. "It is resting between some rocks on the seafloor. The dolphins found it for us. They are so smart! We are watching everything they do on a phone, transmitting from a critter-cam on a dolphin."

"How can we get this done?" frantically cried the hunters, horrified. They were afraid, but they knew that it was up to them to help save the town.

Taylor appeared in the water next to the boat and said, "Come on! We can do it with the help of the dolphins. Follow us, and bring your nets."

Quickly, Taylor advised the dolphins around her, "Do not be afraid, you can go back out to sea or you can choose to help us. We are concerned that if the bomb goes off, it could start a tsunami and destroy everything."

"We'll help," whistled the dolphins.

The hunters were amazed to understand the dolphins for the first time. The hummingbird drone was able to use the crittercam to translate what the dolphins were saying.

"We did not realize that dolphins could talk to each other," the hunters said.

"Yes, like us, they are intelligent beings. Let's go! Follow us to where Katsu and Daisuke have the bomb's location pinpointed," she instructed.

Not one of the dolphins left to go back out to sea despite being hunted by the Japanese people for hundreds of years. They all followed Taylor and Lindsey, and the hunters were right behind them.

Moments later, they were at the bomb being watched over by Katsu and Daisuke.

Daisuke signaled to the dolphin pod and directed, "Everyone grab part of the net and head down here."

The dolphins lined up and each took hold of a piece of the net. They dragged the net down to the bottom of the sea floor, where the bomb was resting. Taylor aimed her bubble gun directly at the bomb, enclosing it in a big bubble.

The bubble slowly lifted in the water, sending little puffs of sand to muddy the water. The sand soon cleared, and they could see the bomb was safely enclosed in the bubble, slightly lifted off the seafloor. The dolphins moved in, wrapping the net under the bomb in its protective bubble wrap.

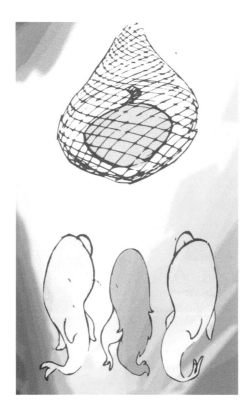

Taylor popped up next to the boat and said, "Okay, time to raise it up!"

The hunters complied, using a winch to raise the bomb up and into the boat, in the same way that they caught dolphins.

"We've got it!" they yelled. All the dolphins whistled with approval, and the hunters smiled at the dolphins.

The low hum of a larger boat engine carrying Mr. Tanaka and the police arrived to defuse the bomb.

The police wore padding and helmets, and they asked everyone to move away.

All of the dolphins swam far out to sea, and Mr. Tanaka and the hunters quickly returned to the shore. Away from the crowd, Lindsey and Taylor followed them to the beach and discretely changed back into their human form.

The only sound heard was the waves crashing on the shore as the silent crowd watched the police's Bomb Squad cautiously approach the small white dinghy cradling the bomb.

Taro met Taylor's eyes. If she was afraid, she didn't show it. What would happen next was anybody's guess.

CHAPTER ELEVEN

Town on a Tightrope

As told by Taylor

As we waited nervously, my thoughts drifted to how I had wound up entangled in this chilling event. When I arrived in Tomo, I thought that the people were cruel and heartless to kill the dolphins. But Taro showed me that most people here are just trying to support their families by working in the hunt. I felt guilty for being so judgmental when I criticized their culture. I didn't understand why they couldn't see this from my point of view. I still believed the dolphin slaughter is wrong, but I was willing to forgive these hunters. When we first began our mission to save the dolphins, it seemed like such a long time ago. I have become so much more confident. I'm proud that I became a leader in finding the bomb.

Now I was about to watch what could be a huge disaster. Tomo's fate hung in the balance, a deadly bomb sitting off its coast. It was possible that we would be engulfed with a huge tsunami wave. I was shaking in my shoes, hoping no one would notice. The four of us had been in some tight situations before, but this one sure was terrifying.

Thinking of our peril made the whole morning flash like a movie before my eyes, from the desperate undersea hunt for the forgotten thing, to the dolphins helping us to raise it up into the boat. Because I was out in the sea, I hadn't realized that half the town was watching and listening through Bobbi's electronics to what we had done.

I suddenly became aware that there was only a deadly silence. Even the birds were not chirping.

Everybody held their breath. You could hear a pin drop. In fact, Lindsey did drop a bobby pin from her hair, and people did hear it.

In the boat far out on the water, we knew that the two officers held tiny tools and were carefully working under the immense pressure. What we did not know was that a drop of sweat fell from the agent's greasy forehead and sizzled onto an exposed red wire, causing a small spark to leap into the air. Both men turned away, shielding their faces from the expected explosion. Seeing them turn away, the crowd gasped and instinctively backed up.

Both agents knew which wire to cut. With shaky hands they cautiously sliced the algae-encrusted wire. They stepped back, turned to the audience, and announced through their radio: "We defused the bomb."

The crowd cheered. As I was jumping up and down, enthusiastically dancing, I lost my footing for a second and fell backward, but a pair of strong arms broke my fall. I turned around to see who had caught me. I locked eyes with my crush, Taro, for a second before I turned away again and blushed. Lindsey, seeing this exchange between me and Taro, poked me hard in the ribs.

"Hey!" I shouted. "Quit making it obvious." It was too late to say anything else; I was already stricken by his big brown eyes and shiny long hair. That boy is so cute, I thought.

I saw that Han the Hunter, standing in the crowd, was overcome by emotion.

Bobbi's hummingbird drones allowed everyone on the beach, no matter their language, to understand each other.

Han said as he looked out to sea, "To think that I never realized before that dolphins were capable of so much. They're almost like people."

I realized at that moment how much had been accomplished by the video and audio from Bobbi's equipment, which so many people had watched. There is a time for fighting for what you believe in, but compassion and understanding were strong tools in allowing the people of Tomo to realize the importance of the dolphins.

The police bomb squad came back to shore and was greeted by yelling and cheering. Lindsey turned to Sophie and Emily. "Thanks for covering the beach," Lindsey said. "In those ACC uniforms, you do look evil. What happened to the real ACC security?"

Emily flashed a knowing grin. "The protesters swam out with Sophie to cut some netting," she said, "while I ran the ACC out of town. Let's just say that we were totally in the zone out there with our special skills."

"No way! Awesome!" Lindsey said.

Emily snickered, "Between my hedgehog quills and the pointy beaks of the winged drones, the ACC agents got the point, in the place that counts."

Mr. Tanaka said to the girls, "We saw on Bobbi's monitor so much of what you

and the dolphins did and said. Our town is grateful to you and the dolphins. From now on, I'm sure dolphins here will have the same rights as people. They really should not be killed."

"You're welcome," I said. "Thank you so much, Mr. Tanaka, for taking the time to watch on the phone. We are grateful, Han, for your help in getting that bomb lifted into your boat."

I paused a moment to glance at the handsome Taro, who was standing next to his dad, Mr. Tanaka. Throughout this adventure, I had come to a new understanding of what people must do to live. Tomo families would not have the money for things they needed without hunting dolphins. I knew that I had to help them find new income sources.

Then I announced, "There is one more thing we must do. We know that the Tomo people live simply and count on the dolphin drive for their income."

I looked at Mr. Tanaka and the other hunters, who nodded. I continued, "As we were told the other day, young people have been leaving Tomo because there is not enough work here. We want to help Tomo with ideas about how to earn income in another way, and we want to help make the town a place where young people can stay to live."

"We're going back to our headquarters for a while," Emily said. "We can get advice from someone we call our Fairy Godmother. But we will be sending you some ideas."

I tried to say goodbye to Taro, but I think my voice came out in only a whisper and that he didn't hear me.

Han said, "We appreciate that you care about what happens to us. You are always welcome here. We, too, will be thinking of what we should do next."

As the Miniworld owners began walking back to the van, Emily said, "I sure will miss it here!"

"Yeah, I think we all will," I said, shaking my head. I personally was finding it a bit hard to start walking away. I was thinking maybe I was leaving someone who might actually understand me.

"I'm just sayin'," said Sophie, "this problem of helping Tomo is hard to solve. One of the villagers reminded me that we raise pigs to eat in our country, and that pigs are smart animals just like dolphins."

Taylor nodded. "For this case, we went all the way to Japan. But eventually we need to tackle animal rights at home. For starters, our farm animals should be able to live better lives. As Miniworld Owners, we should make ethical farming a big priority. We should investigate animal farming that uses inhumane methods."

Lindsey mused, "It is time to seek the advice of our Fairy Godmother. Certainly my nunchucks won't solve this problem of helping Tomo's people, and neither will the rest of our powers. I do have some ideas, though."

"Plus it is time for some ice cream cake," insisted Sophie loudly.

"You can say that again!" said Emily.

"Plus it is time for some ice cream cake!" Sophie repeated.

"Yep," barked Frank. "Let's go back to the van and see if Bobbi will take us to the airport. I get a window seat this time."

Suddenly a boy's voice from behind us called out, "See you later, alligator."

I yelled back to Taro, "See you soon, tycoon."

The girls stared at me.

"What?" I said to them. I was glad I met such a sweet boy but saying good-byes are always hard. "He totally likes me!"

CHAPTER TWELVE

Penguin in Peril

ACC agent Victor Villiny immediately reported to his High Commander that the girls stopped the slaughter by showing the people how smart the dolphins were when they helped save Tomo.

"This is preposterous!" exclaimed the High Commander to his assistant, Villiny. "Those girls have got to be stopped!" In a rage, he shoved all the papers off his desk. "How hard can they be to stop? They're just kids, aren't they?"

"Yes, High Commander," his underling agreed, as he walked around the office picking up the papers. "They are just a few teenaged girls, weaklings. We can start a new dolphin drive. We can move the business up the coast. I have a splendidly evil idea to re-label cans of dolphin as tuna to sell them faster."

"Those horrid girls could just follow us up the coast. Get me one hundred of our most elite ACC agents," the High Commander ordered, his eyes glaring red.

His assistant shook his head. "Sir, we don't have that many."

"Well, then, get me fifty," he bellowed, slamming his fist on his desk.

"We don't have that many, sir," the assistant shrugged.

"Twenty-five," spit out the High Commander.

"Nope."

The High Commander narrowed his eyes at his assistant. "Well how many do we have?"

"Fifteen, sir."

"Okay, fifteen then," the High Commander sighed. "But be quick about it! Those girls have got to go, once and for all!"

In the van to Osaka, Bobbi and the girls told funny stories about Lindsey always being clueless. The girls laughed so hard, that they actually had tears, which the little hummingbird drones collected from the corners of their eyes.

Before they left Japan the girls wanted to check out the aquarium and Bobbi wanted to sketch the jellyfish there. When they arrived at Tempozan Harbor, where the aquarium was located, they were thrilled to experience some Japanese culture.

"Food!" cried the Ultra Twins in unison, hopping up and down.

"I have a yen for dumplings," Taylor grinned.

"You are in luck here," answered Bobbi, who ushered them down a colorful food alley corridor and into a spot serving dumplings. The customers could grind up their own black beans grown in Kyoto. Taylor watched how this was done at a stone grinding mill on a table, then tried it. This provides fresh Kinako powder, which is used in the dumpling.

"The dumpling itself," said Bobbi, "is made from starch from a fern."

"The dumpling is called Warabimochi," said a voice from across the room.

"I know that voice," said Taylor. "Who is over there?"

She peered in the direction of the voice, but whoever it was, was gone.

"You talking to yourself again?" sneered Lindsey, her plate full of Japanese pancakes with vegetables. "You must be losing it."

But Taylor insisted, with a small belch, "There was really someone there."

"Uh-huh," barked Frank as he slurped up pan-fried noodles.

"We don't know anyone in Osaka," Emily reminded them as they finished up and headed to the aquarium.

There was so much to do at the aquarium, that they split up. Bobbi and Frank hiked over to the jellyfish exhibit with Bobbi's drawing notebook. Sophie hung out at the Antarctica area with the big King penguins. Taylor and Nelly went to talk to the Pacific white-sided dolphins, and Emily and Lindsey went to see the giant spider crabs. They agreed to meet in one hour at the Aqua Gate, which was a large, tunnel-shaped tank that you could stand inside.

Taylor and Nelly were the first people to meet back at the spot. Lindsey and Emily showed them pictures of the giant spider crab. Bobbi and Frank eventually showed up a little late.

Of course Sophie was late. "She is probably asking the penguins in the exhibit about their experiences with climate change," Taylor suggested.

After ten more minutes of waiting, they decided to search for Sophie.

They looked for her everywhere. Bobbi texted her in English, Japanese, and finally in penguin.

The group decided to ask the penguins if they had met a blonde girl named Sophie.

One of the penguins said right away, "Sophie was jumped by some ninjas. They were scary, smelled strange, and they were mean."

"You know who this smells of?" Taylor asked Frank. Frank sniffed the air all around the penguin exhibit.

"Villiny!" Frank and Lindsey exclaimed.

"Yes," agreed Taylor, "If he's involved, this can't be friendly."

Only one person would know how to help.

An Urgent Email from Taro

Dear Taylor,

Thank you for the list of ways that our village can move into its future without the dolphin drive. We also have come up with some options and will choose which ones work best for us. It is terrific that the Miniworld website will talk about these ideas further.

I was shocked to hear that Sophie has gone missing from the aquarium in Osaka. My father and I have done some investigation, and we think we discovered what happened to her.

When you went to Osaka, the ACC were waiting for you. Their High Commander was extremely mad and was determined to get rid of at least one of you. The ACC kidnapped Sophie at the aquarium's penguin exhibit and put her in a dolphin shipping container. Records show that ANA airlines sent her from Osaka, Japan to an aquarium called Gigundo Marino in Argentina, South America. I'm sure she had a bumpy ride in that box.

If she survived the trip, the aquarium is likely to put her on display there as a penguin for the visitors. But as you know, if she stays in her animal form too long, she will not be able to change back into a person. So you must hurry!

Let me know how your search for Sophie is going. Tell me how I can help.

Your good friend,

Taro Tanaka

Visit the Miniworld Website!

https://miniworld.net/

As you probably have been able to figure out, *The Dolphin Rescue* is a story about what the future might be like if we all worked together. The story is about our personal ideas, the world's problems, and how to change things for the better.

When we work together, our energy is shared. We can create a new world. We must be confident and stand up to those who are hurting animals.

We hope you like Miniworld, and that you, too, believe that animals should be treated humanely.

Please visit our website, https://miniworld.net/, to learn more about animals and to have fun with us.